# Princess Rani

First published in 2008
by Wayland

This paperback edition published in 2009





Wayland
338 Euston Road
London NW1 3BH

Wayland Australia
Level 17/207 Kent Street
Sydney, NSW 2000





Series Editor: Louise John
Editor: Katie Powell
Cover design: Paul Cherrill
Design: D.R.ink
Consultant: Shirley Bickler

A CIP catalogue record for this book is available from the British Library.

ISBN 9780750255370 (hbk)
ISBN 9780750255417 (pbk)

Printed in China

Wayland is a division of Hachette Children's Books,
an Hachette Livre UK Company

www.hachettelivre.co.uk

# Princess Rani

Written by Penny Dolan
Illustrated by Bruno Robert

WAYLAND

Rani was a circus elephant.
She liked to walk into
the Big Top dressed up like
a princess.

Vish was her keeper. He rode on her back dressed up like a prince.

But when the show was over, Vish looked after Rani.

Every day he got Rani her food.

Rani liked to eat lots of
grass, leaves and branches.

She had a big tummy to fill.

"That elephant costs too much money!" grumbled Carlo.

"Maybe I don't need an elephant in my circus."

Vish stroked Rani's
big ears.

"Never mind, Rani," he told her. "I'm sure someone will want us."

"Look! Over there!" called Lola Fanola, suddenly.

Smoke was coming from the Big Top.

“Where are the buckets?”
cried Carlo.

“They’re all inside the Big Top,” said Joey the Juggler.

“Quick, Rani! The pond’s over here!” said Vish.

Rani dipped her trunk into the pond, and she sucked in water.

Then, Rani blew it out over the fire. WHOOSH!

She got more and
more water.

WHOOSH! WHOOSH!
At last the fire was out.

"Well done, Rani!" cried Carlo.

"I do need an elephant in my circus, after all!"

**START READING** is a series of highly enjoyable books for beginner readers. **The books have been carefully graded to match the Book Bands widely used in schools.** This enables readers to be sure they choose books that match their own reading ability.

**Look out for the Band colour on the book in our Start Reading logo.**

The Bands are:

**START READING** books can be read independently or shared with an adult. They promote the enjoyment of reading through satisfying stories supported by fun illustrations.

**Penny Dolan** had great fun writing about Carlo's Circus, because she could pretend she was an expert juggler, brave trapeze artist, cheeky clown and an amazing elephant rider – even though she's definitely not!

**Bruno Robert** lives and works in Normandy, France, where he was born. He always wanted to draw and play with colours. When he is illustrating a story like this one, he likes to think of a bright and colourful world that is full of humour.